Be Honest,

by Molly Smith • illustrated by Marc Monés

"Don't let the balloon touch the floor, Jess!" said my brother Will.

I dove across the room to save it.

I hit the balloon. The balloon went up.
Then I hit the vase. The vase went down.

Crack! The vase broke on the floor.
"Oh no!" cried Will. "Mom is going to be
so mad."

"What should we do?" I asked. "We shouldn't have been playing that game in here."

"Let's try to glue it back together before Mom sees it," said Will.

I picked up the rest of the vase and we brought it to my room. Then we heard Mom.

"Kids!" she called. "Lunch is ready!"

I quickly put the broken vase in my closet and we ran to the kitchen.

"What were you two up to?" she asked.

"NOTHING!" we said at the same time.

Then Mom went into the other room.
Will and I held our breath.

"Where is the blue vase?" she asked.

My heart was beating fast.

I thought of all the excuses I could give.

"I broke it!" I blurted out.
"We were playing with the balloon and I knocked over the vase. Are you mad?"

"No, I'm not mad," said Mom.

"I'm proud of you for being honest with me."

"I'm really sorry, Mom," I said.

"It's okay," she said. "Accidents happen.
Now let's take a look at that vase."

"We can fix the vase," Mom said.
"But trust is much harder to fix
when it's broken."